EMPTY SOUL

A DIRTY SOULS SPIN OFF

EMMA CREED

Empty Soul
Copyright 2021 by Emma Creed
All Rights Reserved
First Edition

No part of this book may be reproduced or transmitted in any form or by any means, electronic or mechanical, including photocopying, recording, or by any information storage and retrieval system without written permission of the author, except for the use of brief quotations in a book review.

This is a work of fiction. Names, characters, businesses, places, events and incidents are either the product of the author's imagination or used in a fictitious manner. Any resemblance to actual persons, living or dead, actual events, or locales is entirely coincidental. The use of any real company and/or product names is for literary effect only. All other trademarks and copyrights are the property of their respective owners.

Cover design by: Rebel Ink Co
Interior design by: Rebel Ink Co
Photographer: Darren Birks
Model: Darren Birks
Editing by: Sassi's Editing Services

'Bound not by blood but loyalty.
We live, we ride, and we die
by our own laws'

PROLOGUE
LEVI

"You're too fuckin' perfect," I growl when I feel her toned thighs tighten around my waist. My fingers squeeze her ass cheeks, and I control the pace as I slam her body down hard on my cock. I want her to take every inch of me. I want her to still be feeling me inside her when she leaves me and goes to work.

"Holy fuck, Levi," she breathes against my jaw, gripping my hair with desperate hands. Beth's considerate, she'll be worrying about waking up Ryan in the room next door or some shit. But I don't give a fuck if we wake the whole damn town because right now, I want everyone in Springdale to know that Beth Miller's tight little pussy is squeezing the life out of my cock.

She slides her hands down my neck, her nails pressing into my shoulders as she grinds her orgasm out on me. Thrusting her hips to her own rhythm. While I grab at her flesh trying to stay grounded and empty my load deep inside that perfect pussy.

It always happens like this with us. That dirty as sin smile that twitches on my pretty girl's face just as she gives herself up to me is too fucking sexy to hold off on.

"You're gonna make me late," she teases, that warm, wet

pussy still clenching at my cock and making me want to take her all over again.

"I'm sure Reena will understand." I shift fast, flipping our bodies and laying her back on the mattress. Then after I've pinned her wrists above her head, I kiss the ever living shit out of those sweet lips.

"I promised I'd be in for the breakfast rush." She fights against me feebly, and I slide my nose along her jaw until my mouth finds her ear.

"Quit," I whisper.

"I can't quit my job, Levi, I need to work," she protests and I can't see it, but I know she's rolling her eyes at me.

"Well at least get a job you enjoy, you hate working in that coffee place."

"I got to pay my way now I'm an adult," she reminds me, and when I pull back I see her sad smile. I hate it.

Beth's family struggle, she's one of six siblings whose Father's a pastor and relies far too much on 'God's will' to get them by.

Things are tight in the Miller household.

"You know I'm gonna put a ring on your finger someday soon," I promise, clenching her fingers between mine.

"You really think my daddy will ever allow that?" Her eyes widen doubtfully. "His sweet, innocent little Beth sinning with one of the town's bad boy bikers."

"I don't give two fucks what your daddy says, darlin'. We're written in the stars you and me. You're mine, always have been, always will be. You..." I scrape my teeth over the skin on her neck before I pull my head back and look down at her, "...are everything I've ever wanted, and Levi-fucking-Bridges always gets what he wants."

"Well then Levi-fucking-Bridges, grow a set of balls and go ask him." She stretches up to kiss me on the lips before giving me the slip, ducking her body under my arm.

"You know I'm gonna do things his way. I'll even ask him. Once I got my own place and I can offer you shit." I roll on to my side, propping my head in my hand and watching her pulling on her clothes.

"Since I got patched I've been putting money aside, I'm gonna getcha a place just like your mom and dad's, and we're gonna fill it up with hell raisers."

"Yeah?" She stops buttoning up her shirt and smiles back at me dreamily.

"Absolutely," I promise.

God, I love her, can't remember past a time when I didn't.

"Well..." she slides her cowboy boots up over her jeans before crawling back on top of me.

"You better make sure you got a hell of a speech for my father. The outlaw and the pastor's daughter sounds a lot like a romantic tragedy to me."

I fist her hair in my hand and force her mouth onto mine, my tongue slipping between her lips and rolling lazily around hers before I pull away again.

"You better get outta here before I pin you back down and give your daddy a reason to make me marry you," I warn.

"You're going straight to hell, Levi Bridges," she giggles.

And as it turns out my girl was right, because hell is exactly where I am when I open my eyes.

The room smells like weed and bad fucking choices, my mouth is dry and the throbbing in my temples reminds me of all the vodka I knocked back last night.

I manage to sit up on the edge of the mattress, scrubbing my face before I assess the mess of my situation. I've been staying here at the Colorado Charter for over a week now, and these brothers party way too fucking hard.

There's a half empty bottle on the nightstand and I knock a mouthful back before locating my cut, patting down the pockets and finding my smokes.

"Morning'."

I've just lit up when I hear the voice come from behind me. I don't wanna turn and look, it don't matter how pissed or hungover I am, I know the person I'll see ain't gonna be the one I want it to be.

"You okay, baby?" the blonde bitch asks, helping herself to the bottle in my hand.

"I gotta take a shower." My voice comes out scratchy as I stand up and head for the bathroom. "Make sure you're gone by the time I get out," I call back at her.

The set up they got here in Colorado is much nicer than the other Charters. Lakeside cabins, plenty of space. Pussy practically crawling at your feet. I could have settled here after I left Utah but it was far too close, so I chose to go nomad instead.

When I left my home Charter, I thought I'd leave all the grief and guilt there too. But the truth is, I carry those fuckers around with me no matter how far I get away from Springdale.

When I'm done scrubbing off last night's sins in the shower I hear my phone ringing, so I quickly tuck a towel around my waist and rush back to the bedroom to pick it up.

"Yep?" I answer when I see Declan's name flash up. He's Prez of the Utah Charter now. Me, him and Ryan were all fucking solid growing up.

"What's up?"

"I'm just hanging at Jimmer's Charter in Colorado. I helped them out on a run a few days ago. Everything calm out your way?"

"Yeah, we ain't got no hassle, but there is a reason I called you, brother." I hear the drop in his tone and know it's gonna be bad. His old man stepped down as Prez a few years ago, if anything's happened to him, Dec is gonna be devastated.

"Look, you can't tell Mia I told you this but…" he holds off like he doesn't wanna finish, and that gets me even more suspicious. What the fuck would Dec's little sister care about what he tells me?

Unless…

Beth!

Mia and Beth have been best friends since they were in kindergarten.

"What? What doesn't Mia want me to know?" I try my best not to sound irritated when I respond.

"That Beth's getting married this weekend." Dec's words hit me like a punch to the guts, and I drop on to the bed and stare up at the ceiling. My heart feeling like it just got fucking swallowed.

"Levi, you still there?" Dec's voice reminds me that he's still on the line.

"I'm here."

"I wasn't gonna call you, I didn't wanna fuck with your head. But I just… I know what she meant to you and, well, it didn't feel right not to tell ya."

"I appreciate that," I tell him, trying to keep myself together when all I wanna do is put my fist through the fucking wall.

"Who?" I ask the question, even though I know I don't really want the answer. I don't wanna know what cunt gets to have her now. What asshole will be Beth's fucking husband.

"You remember Laurie Preston?"

"Laurie Preston, that fucking weasel? You kidding me with this shit?"

"Yeah, well that fucking weasel came back to town from law school with a degree and swept your bitch right off her heels."

I close my eyes and see her fucking face, that smile, those eyes, and they tear right through my fucking heart.

"I'm sorry, man," Dec sounds genuine. He's always had my back, despite all the shit that happened back home being my fault.

"Don't be sorry." I snap my eyes open when reality fucking hits me, and I sit up, a sudden surge of adrenaline pumping the blood under my skin.

Beth Miller is fucking mine, and for five years I've only been pretending that it could ever be any other way.

"Don't be sorry, brother, because there ain't gonna be no fuckin' wedding," I tell Declan.

I left town five years ago because I convinced myself I was doing the right thing by my girl. I've hurt, I've suffered, and despite that I've stayed away. But hearing those fucking words, the thought of someone else owning those pretty smiles for life... well that shit just kicked me in the face with a reality check.

I ain't gonna stand back and let some other guy take what should always have fucking been mine.

"What do you mean?" Dec asks, the hard bastard actually sounds a little nervous.

"I'm coming home, Prez. And you're gonna have to break it to that sister of yours that there ain't no way her best friend's walking up that aisle."

I hang up, throw on last night's clothes and pack up my shit. Then hopping on my bike, I kickstart the engine and head back to Springdale. To face all the shit I ran away from five years ago... and to claim what's fucking mine.

Chapter 1
BETH

"You look fucking on fire," Mia tells me when I step out of the dressing room. My crazy best friend looks out of place here, slouched back with her feet up on the fancy chaise lounge that's beneath the window of Marie's bridal boutique.

"Breathtaking," Marie says before taking her eyes away from me to look disapprovingly at Mia for her foul language.

"Laurie's eyes are gonna fall out of his sockets when you make your way up that aisle," she promises, planting a kiss against my cheek. "And his cock's gonna..." I throw Mia a look before she can finish that sentence.

Marie and my mom had been best friends for as long as I can remember. She only has sons herself, and with Mom now no longer with us, I know Marie has been planning this dress for way longer than the six months' notice I gave her to make it.

A loud rumbling noise from the street outside makes my stomach automatically flip. It's pathetic how things like that still provoke a reaction from me. Especially since Springdale is home to the Dirty Souls, who Mia's brother leads, and bikes are seen and heard a lot.

"Are you wearing your hair up or down?" Marie pulls me back into the moment, lifting the hair off my neck and holding it loosely while we both look in the mirror. Honestly, I haven't even thought about how I'll wear my hair, that, and this dress are about the only things I do have to think about so you'd think I'd give them more attention.

Laurie's mom seems to have taken on the organization of everything else. Not that I have a problem with it. I find the whole thing completely overwhelming.

"Holy fucking shit!" The shock in Mia's voice causes me to turn and look over my shoulder, and just as Marie is about to curse her for her language again, she freezes into the same shocked silence that's taken hold of me.

I can't be seeing what I think I am. It can't be Levi Bridges, all six-foot-two-inches of the man who broke my heart marching across the street, eyes focused like he's charging into battle. Because if it is, the poor fragile heart I've barely stitched back together won't survive what happens next. And when the door pulls open and that's exactly who steps inside, in one sharp tug all those stitches come loose.

"You've got some nerve, Bridges," Mia stands up and charges for him, but he pays her no attention. His harsh brown eyes too focused on staring into mine, knocking the air out of my lungs and making my legs threaten to buckle beneath me.

"Levi," the name falls from my lips in a weak whisper and every muscle in my body twitches to run at him.

But hell if I'll give into it. Heartbreak and stubbornness somehow pull their shit together and keep me rooted to the spot. "What are you doing in town?" I do my best to sound calm and unfazed.

"I knew Dec wouldn't keep his mouth shut. I'm gonna kill him," Mia fumes, pacing in front of us like a rabid dog, but I can't focus on anything other than the man standing in front of me.

The years haven't changed Levi Bridges, he's still the most beautiful man I've ever seen. Dark hair, cut short at the sides and flopping over his forehead, an impressive thick beard, and those eyes that can make a girl flutter with more than just her lashes. I watch him inhale through his nostrils as his pupils take me in and for just a heartbeat, all that confidence he strode in here with, slips away.

"I need a word." He drops his eyes to the floor and clears his throat.

"A word," I catch my breath then actually laugh when I realize what he just said. "You left town five years ago without words, Levi, what's the use in them now?"

"You need to get back on your bike and..." Mia starts, but Marie quickly launches towards her and ushers her away.

"Beth, I really need to speak with you." There's a warning in his tone and I have to swallow back tears when I hear him say my name. I'm not strong enough for this, five years ago when Levi rode out of town, he took all my hopes and dreams with him and now after all this time, when I'm just about to let all that go, he has the nerve to turn up and want to talk about it.

"There's nothing you've got to say that I want to hear." I pull up the dress I'm wearing so I don't trip, and rush towards the changing room to get away from him.

Once inside, I pull the curtain closed and suck in a huge breath. My corset suddenly feels too tight, like I can't take in enough oxygen and I quickly fumble behind me to try and loosen the ribbons.

"Shit," I jump, when the curtain rips open, and Levi steps inside before pulling it back across and trapping us in the tiny space. His tall, sturdy body overpowers mine as I look up at him and feel all my willpower drain into a shameful pool in my panties.

"Just give me a few minutes." His voice sounds less authoritative, almost pleading, and the deep bass of it makes my bones shudder.

"I gave you five years," I manage, somehow holding his stare and hoping that I emanate hate instead of hurt.

His strong arm stretches over my shoulder, his palm resting

on the wall behind me, and that familiar scent of leather and tobacco drifts up through my nostrils and makes it almost impossible not to react.

I'm trapped between him and the wall, wondering why the hell Mia and Marie haven't intervened? And when the rough, callous thumb of his other hand strokes along my cheek I close my eyes and allow myself a second of weakness. To breathe him in, to sink into his touch and let myself feel whole again.

"Do you love him?" Levi's voice cracks with a weakness of its own, and I'm too scared to open my eyes and answer him. This man, no matter how much time or distance has been put between us, knows me. He knows me better than anyone else ever has or ever will.

"Yes," I whisper back, swallowing the lump that's wedged in my throat.

"Open your eyes, darlin'," Levi whispers, but I shake my head keeping them tightly closed.

"Open your eyes and look at me," he demands.

I suddenly shoot them open and use all the power left inside me to blaze all the hell he's put me through deep into his soul.

"Tell me you love him." He narrows his eyes and I feel all his tension in the hand he's using to cradle my face. The traction between us draws like a magnet. But I fight it, for all the years he's been gone and the mess he left behind. I fucking fight it.

"I. Love. Him." I say the words slowly because I want them to hurt him, even though they feel empty to me now. Less than five minutes back in Levi's presence has taught me that I've spent the last twelve months kidding myself with Laurie.

I can't love him... I don't know how I ever thought I could have, not while my heart was still so raw for this man.

My lips tremble when his hand slides down my neck, making a delicate arch around my throat. And when his heavy body presses into mine, my back connects with the wall he's leaning against and leaves no more space between us.

I feel my pulse beat fast against his fingertips, memories of the way they used to touch me making my pussy respond in a way he doesn't deserve. And when he lowers his head closer to mine, I realize there's no escaping him.

I don't think I even want to anymore.

The tip of his nose slides along my jaw until his lips brush against my ear.

"I don't believe you." His dark whisper ricochets through my body making me want to kiss him and beat the crap out of him at the same time for all the desperation he's putting inside me.

"Levi, you need to leave." I hear the shake in my voice, knowing that he'll hear it too. Jesus, I feel like I'm going to pass out. The shock of him being here, the heat between us, it's all too much to withstand in such a small space.

"I lost my way for a while, but I'm back now and there ain't gonna be no fucking wedding," he tells me. Igniting flames of fury inside my stomach.

How dare he.

"So, you take off this pretty white dress, and we're gonna stop pretending that you could ever belong to anyone else." His teeth graze my earlobe as he pulls away from me, causing a static heat to spread beneath my skin. The whoosh of the curtain as it draws open brings me back to earth again and Levi casually steps out onto the shop floor, nodding his head at a furious looking Mia and a shocked Marie before he strolls out the door, crosses the street, and mounts his bike.

"Well things just livened back up in Springdale," Marie smiles to herself, as the three of us watch him pull away.

CHAPTER 2
LEVI

I park my bike outside the clubhouse and as I step inside, I get hit with familiar comfort and sinking guilt all at the same time.

My old clubhouse ain't as fancy as the one back in Colorado, we do business on a much smaller scale around here, but for me, this place will always be home.

It's the middle of the day, so the place is dead and when I look around the empty bar room, I'm plagued by all the memories that remind me exactly why I left.

"Dec in his office?" I check with the woman who's cleaning up the bar. I know he's here somewhere, his bike was the only one parked out front.

"Sure is, honey." She smiles back at me, and I nod my gratitude at her before making my way up the stairs to find him.

I knock on the door and when he calls me inside, I find him sitting at his desk, some hot little slut resting on his lap and playing with his hair.

"Go down and see if Helen needs any help," Dec taps her on the ass and she slides off his lap, smiling at me as she passes through the door.

I wait until she's gone before stepping forward and tossing a brown envelope on the desk.

"That's from Jimmer, says there's plenty more of it coming if we can keep it stored. Him and the boys are bringing up the next haul when they travel up for Troj's fight." Dec slides the envelope full of cash across the old scratched surface and straight into his top draw before looking back up at me judgingly.

He's got no intention in talking club business right now.

"Mia called," he informs me, looking pissed.

"Thought she might." I scratch the back of my neck awkwardly then take a seat. Kicking up my feet on the desk and lighting myself a smoke.

Dec lets out a long, exhausted breath and shakes his head in disapproval.

"Out with it." I roll my eyes and prepare for his lecture, the guy's one of my oldest friends. *If he can't say it to me, ain't no one who can.*

"Hey," he shows me his palms, "I ain't claiming to be no female expert, but even I know you can't quit on a relationship like the one you did, give no explanation, then rock back up all alpha five years later." He laughs to himself before lighting up a cigarette of his own and leaning back in his leather chair.

"I had my reasons for leaving." I stare at the picture Dec's got on his desk, the one of me, him and Ryan on the day Dec's Pop patched us all in.

It hurts like hell knowing he ain't with us no more, but it's a whole different kind of agony knowing it's all my fault.

"I had Helen make you up a room, it's yours for as long as you need it, brother." Dec must pick up on my pain and he spares me by quickly changing the subject.

"Just think about what you're doing before you start fucking shit up for Beth. She's Mia's best friend, and the last thing I need is my sister bitchin' in my ear."

"Who's running things around here?" I release a long stream of smoke into the air and snigger back at him.

"You know how protective Mia is, and if you were any other

fucker and I didn't know what she meant to ya, I'd be running you out of town myself. Beth's a good girl. She deserves to be happy," he warns.

"Which is why she ain't marrying that lawyer, Dec, she don't love him. And if she didn't already know it. I just proved it to her. It's all still there between us, everything I should never have ran out on. She belongs with me and I'm gonna make her see it."

"Just hope you ain't too late." Dec stands up and rounds his desk. "Come on let's go get a drink, you can tell me about your game plan."

I'm only on my second beer when the bar door swings open and a furious Mia storms right at me. Since we were kids, me and her have always had that love hate thing going on, I guess she's just all about the hate these days.

"You selfish cu…"

"Woooh," Dec stands up and puts himself between us, preventing the little firecracker from unleashing on me.

Mia's a hot little thing, long blonde hair, a cute petite frame and a whole lot of attitude. I'll bet half the brothers in this Charter have thought about being up in her business. But not one of 'em who value their nut sacks would ever act on it.

"Move out of my way, shit face, this is just as much your fault as it is his. You should never have told him." Mia stabs a finger deep into the center of her brother's chest.

"Don't forget where you are and who you're speaking to," he reminds her.

Dec's a hard bastard, he didn't step up into his pop's role as Prez at such a young age by being a pushover, but when it comes to Mia…

"Well move out of my way and let me at him," Mia seethes.

And Dec's shoulders sag as he steps aside, shooting me an apologetic smile.

"How dare you think you can ride back into this town after all these years and ruin this." All of her attention is centered on me now. There ain't nothing she's gonna tell me that I don't already know.

Am I being unreasonable?

Yes.

Am I being selfish?

Yes.

Am I gonna let that stop me?

Hell no!

I thought about this the whole ride out here. It's all I've thought about since Dec told me about the wedding.

No one's gonna stop me from being with my girl, not even my own self-pity. I've made plenty of bad decisions but I'm clear on this. I'm the one who's meant to make Beth Miller happy.

"She doesn't love him," I shrug, taking a sip from my beer. "You're her best friend, you should know that," I point out, and it knocks the sharp-tongued little minx off guard for a few seconds.

"Well… Laurie is reliable, he loves her. And he didn't leave her with a broken heart," she throws back at me, before taking the shot that Helen offers her over the bar and downing it.

She lets the liquid burn her throat and settle in her stomach before she continues.

"Look, Levi," she says my name like it's venom dripping off her lips, "Beth's got a good thing with Laurie, he's crazy about her. What you're doing here isn't fair and I swear to god if you ruin it for her, I'll tie you up outside this bar by your balls," she promises, before spinning on her heels and storming back out again.

"Well, that's me told." I wait until she's out of sight before I look back at Dec, he's got a proud smile on his face, he knows ain't no one ever gonna fuck with that little sister of his.

"I don't wanna get ya into shit with the boss but I'm gonna need you to tell me where Beth lives now, I only got a few days and I need to talk her out of this bullshit."

"You know exactly where to find her." Dec chuckles to himself.

"You mean she's still living at home?" I check, confused, I can't be hearing him right.

"Hell yeah, her and scholar boy are doing things proper, like you'd expect a pastor's daughter to. He's had her a brand new house built up on Craggs hill, glass fuckin' walls and all that fancy shit. Place sticks out like a dick in a hoe bar.

I nod my head back slowly, taking in everything he's telling me. Sounds like Laurie's got a lot to offer.

Beth's a hard worker, she's been helping her parents take care of her siblings for as long as I can remember. She deserves a nice house and all the nice shit he can give her.

Maybe I'm an asshole for wanting to snatch all that away. For expecting her to give all that up for the little I got to offer.

"I gotta go talk to her," I stand up from the stool I'm resting on and finish what's left in my bottle.

"You got some balls turning up on the doorstep of the man whose daughter's heart you broke, Bridges," Dec snuffles a laugh at me.

Me and this guy have done some crazy shit together, he knows what I'm capable of.

"Trust me. I'm more worried about your sister than I am Beth's old man." I pat him on the back and head out, there's somewhere I need to visit before I get to the Millers' place.

The front yard is overgrown, the mailbox rusty and hanging at a slope, and the porch floor is rotten. The place needs a lot of work to be liveable. It needed a lot of work back when I put the deposit down on it all those years ago.

I planned for me and Beth to do that together. I was never one for all that DIY shit, but I know the club would have pulled together and helped out. Beth would have picked out all the important stuff that made it a home and we would have been happy here.

The place is still ours, even though she never knew about it. It was gonna be a surprise. How could a girl say no to a guy when you get down on your knee outside a house you just bought her.

But looking at it now, it don't seem like much of a gesture. Not compared to a luxury three story with a view… I drove past Craggs hill on the way out here to check it out.

I've kept up with the mortgage payments for all these years, never once thought about selling up. Perhaps I always knew that one day I'd find the guts to pull my shit together and come back here. I just spent too long worrying about it hurting. I was in a bad place when I left. Numb of anything other than hate, and Beth deserved more than that.

Springdale never did feel right after we lost Ryan, didn't matter how many of those Fallen Saints we made bleed, or the fact me and Dec made the one that took him from us pay with his life. The grief still lingered. I still feel it now festering in the air, crawling under my skin and eating away at my conscience.

As boys, this town was our playground, our fathers the ones who ruled it. We were born to be Dirty Souls, and getting through our prospect probation was a path we travelled together.

Being back here without Ryan riding beside me will never feel right. I'll always carry the burden of the choices I made the night he was taken. But if he were here now, he'd be telling me that I'm doing the right thing. That it's time to heal. And to do that, I'm gonna need Beth to give me the second chance I don't deserve.

CHAPTER 3
BETH

"Tristan you are not to leave this house until you've finished that homework," I yell at my brother, hearing the front door slam before I've even finished my sentence. Frustration rages through me, especially when the smoke alarm starts to beep and I realize I'm burning the chicken under the grill.

"Darn and blast it," I moan, grabbing a dry cloth and pulling it out the oven, slamming the boiling hot tray onto the counter.

Everything around me has been thrown into turmoil since this afternoon. I can't think straight enough to do the simplest tasks.

"You okay, Beth?" my sister Annie looks up from the text book she's studying at the kitchen table for her finals.

"Fine, I'm just…" I struggle to come up with something to tell her.

"Nervous about the wedding," she smiles sympathetically. She's been the one I've dragged along to all of Cynthia's pre-wedding appointments with me. Mia was never an option, that girl can't hold her tongue well enough to help me cope with Laurie's mom.

"I'm nervous too, at least you get to choose your dress. My bridesmaid's dress is hideous, half the town's gonna be there to laugh at me in it." Annie tries to make me feel better, but it fails.

I smile back at her apologetically before trying to salvage the mess I'm making of dinner.

"Beth, Zach isn't sharing, it's my turn on the Xbox."

"Neither of you should be on the damn thing anyway," I remind them, knowing how Father gets about the boys playing video games on school nights. He'll be home any minute, and the last thing they want is for him to confiscate it again.

My cell starts to vibrate among all the chaos and I quickly answer, pressing it to my ear while I head over to the refrigerator.

"How's the mad house?" The sound of Laurie's voice makes me stop what I'm doing, and suddenly I feel awful. I haven't thought about him once since Levi stormed into Marie's and blew a hole into the ground beneath me.

"Crazy as ever," I answer, hoping he doesn't sense the guilt in my voice, maybe I'm just being paranoid.

"Listen, baby, I know I said we could catch that movie tonight but I'm pretty tied up here at work," he explains, sounding guilty himself.

"It's fine," I answer, actually relieved at not having the pressure of seeing him tonight. I still haven't decided if I should tell him that Levi's back in town. Laurie, like everyone else in town, knows how much I hurt when he left.

"You excited about tomorrow?" he asks, and I imagine a smile pulling on to his handsome face. He's such a different kind of handsome to Levi, Laurie is attractive in a clean-cut, classic kind of way.

"Tomorrow?" I rack my brain trying to figure what he's talking about. God if I've got to go to another planning meeting with his mother, I swear I'll go crazy.

"Your bachelorette party," he laughs down the phone. "You can't have forgotten."

"No, of course not," I laugh back nervously, taking out some salad stuff and starting to put together the lunch bags for tomorrow.

"Well, I'm sure Mia's got something sinful planned for you," he says sarcastically.

"Yeah, she's been looking forward to it."

"Listen, I gotta go, baby, I'm about to step into a meeting with a client. I love you."

"Love you too," I tell him back, and realize that there's no meaning behind the words I just gave him, I don't think there ever has been. It's always been an automatic response. Like a please or a thank you.

And that realization hits me like a car wreck as I hang up the phone.

I don't have time to dwell on it though, not while kids need feeding.

Father marches through the door about a half an hour later with a much less confident Tristan trailing behind him. Father gives him a clip across the back of his head before he heads straight for the basin to wash up.

"Found him spying in a tree outside Mrs. Reynolds," Father explains looking angry.

"Tristan, what were you doing there?" I ask, surprised.

"More like what was *he* doing there," Tristan looks at Father spitefully. "Momma's only been gone three years and he's trying to replace her. This wouldn't be happening if you weren't marrying Laurie." It surprises me when he turns his anger on me, angry tears forming in his eyes before he rushes out the room. He's the oldest of my brothers and rarely shows any emotions.

"What's all that about?" I look to Dad who shrugs back and takes his seat at the table.

"It's no secret that I've been spending time in Janice's company. We're both widowers and she's been chipping in around here plenty to pick up your slack."

"Slack? Dad, the only times I'm not here to put a dinner on

this table is when I'm working," I point out. "Things are gonna change around here after the wedding and you have to be ready. I can still help out where I can but…"

"I won't be made to feel guilty for enjoying some female company," he barks back defensively. I'm just about to argue that that's not the point I'm trying to make, but a loud knock at the door interrupts.

"I got it," Annie races from the table, escaping the awkwardness, and I stare at Father, wishing he would ease up a little.

"Ummm, Beth, there's a guy here to see you," Annie calls out from the hall and butterflies instantly attack my stomach. I know exactly who it's going to be.

"Shall I invite him in?"

"No, I'm coming out." I rush past Father and head for the door, gesturing a dreamy eyed Annie away with my head.

Levi stands on the porch, his hand wrapped around the back of his neck and an awkward look on his face, and I let my eyes move over him for a few seconds more than I should. Rugged and fucking delicious, he's everything that should make a woman turn and run. And yet I crave him, despite all the pain he's put me through I still fucking crave him.

"What are you doing here?" I quickly move outside and shut the door behind me. I don't want this to be a big deal and if Dad knows it's Levi that's come calling, this WILL be a big deal.

"I came to ask you if you wanted to take a ride, like old times." He hits me with that bad boy grin that makes me want to throw my body at him, still, I manage to hold off.

Father's always telling us how the lord works in mysterious ways, that he sends temptation to test us. And Levi Bridges looking this damn good on my doorstep has certainly been sent to try me.

"I can't… I mean I won't. Levi, I'm engaged, I'm getting married in six days. You need to accept that," I whisper. Jesus, if the neighbors see him out here, word will spread fast. The entire town will be talking about us, again.

"No, you ain't," Levi shakes his head, that confident smile still fixed on his face.

"This isn't a joke, you can't expect me to just cancel a wedding because you decided you made a mistake." The smile drops from his face and when he reaches out and grabs one of my hands, pulling me closer to him, I nervously glance down the street and check that no one can see.

"Yeah, I made a mistake," he admits. "I realize that now, and I ain't gonna let you do the same. I know he's got you a big house and money but…"

"Whoa…" I immediately yank myself out of his grasp. "You think that's why I said yes to him?" I bite back, suddenly feeling hurt. "I'm marrying Laurie because he's a good person. He's kind, he loves me… And, I love him." I cross my arms over my chest and stare back hard. I need to be strong. This has to end here. Levi needs to get the hell out of town.

The smirk slides back on to Levi's lips and I watch weakly as his tongue, agonizingly slowly, wets his lips.

"Say that a few more times, darlin', you might convince yourself it's true." He backs up off the porch, and it's not until he turns his back on me that I manage to breathe. My feet remain stuck to the doorstep, watching him straddle his saddle, and he stares right back at me as he kickstarts his bike. The engine roaring to life, and filling my stomach with heat as he nods me a goodbye that promises I'll be seeing him again.

CHAPTER 4

LEVI

"Where's the shit, Milo?" I pin the fucker to the floor by his throat while Skinner, Dec's Sgt in arms, and Locke turn the place upside down. Dec stands over the sorry piece of shit, staring down his nose and waiting for his answer.

Last night, this scumbag took advantage of Soul hospitality. He drank from our bar, snorted our blow from a club whore's ass before he fucked her in it, and to show us his gratitude, he stole from us.

"It was just a few grams. You were handing that stuff out for free last night. I thought it would be cool." He holds his hands up and Dec slowly crushes his fingers under his boot.

"Where's the shit, Milo?" he repeats my question, and I feel the kid trembling. He's in way over his head. But anyone who fucks with our club learns the hard way.

"It's gone, I sold it on," he admits. "You know how hard it is to score around here." The sweat drips out of his pores as he shakes under my grip.

"It's hard to score in this town, Milo, because we make it that way," Dec points out, crouching down. "Drugs in Springdale is bad news for the club. Fingers start getting pointed and heat starts to spread."

The Souls have the same policy with all of our Charters, we

protect our hometowns. We keep the streets that surround us clean. Idiots like Milo jeopardize all that hard work.

"I'm feeling generous today. So, I'm gonna take the cash you made from selling my shit, and you're gonna take a lesson from Levi here, for your disrespect." Dec straightens up and gives me the nod.

I leave Milo's bungalow half an hour later, with bruised knuckles, and feeling a little sorry for Milo. He probably got a little more than he actually deserved due to my state of mind.

Skinner had to intervene and pull me off the useless piece of shit, because unleashing all the anger that's been building up since I got back here felt too fucking good. There was a moment when even I didn't think I'd stop.

"Feel better?" Dec smiles at me as we hop on our bikes.

"Nah," I shake my head. Ain't no point lying to him.

"Well, I promised Mia I'd keep you occupied tonight, she wants Beth's bachelorette party to go without a hitch. You wanna go grab a few at Montel's? I got some business to take care of with Stevie, but we could shoot some pool and chill after."

Montel's was where we always hung out when we were younger. The club co-own the place, and we were always guaranteed to get served back in the day. Distraction is exactly what I need right now because I'm all out of ideas on how I'm gonna make Beth see sense. I've even thought about making Laurie disappear. Grimm back in Colorado is an expert in the field.

But eliminating Laurie ain't gonna resolve the fact that I've lost my girl's trust. I broke her heart and that's something I might have to pay a lifelong price for.

"Sounds good," I nod back at Dec, starting up my bike and following him back into town until we reach the bar.

It's getting late and Skinner and Locke have bailed on us to take some pussy back to the club. Dec's off his face, and I've stayed sober to cover his ass. Our Prez doesn't need his Sgt in arms while I'm around. I've lost one best friend, ain't no way I'll be losing another anytime soon.

The bar's still busy, this dive is the liveliest place in Springdale, other than the club, and I've spotted a few bitches trying to get our attention from the other side of the room, not that it makes any difference. I learned pretty quickly after leaving town that I was never gonna fuck Beth out of my head. She's been like a curse since the day I left her, and I ain't ready to accept an option where I can't get her back.

What may come across to her as arrogant and confident, in reality is desperation.

"You're not drinking, bud, why ain't ya drinking?" Dec slurs, hitting back another shot.

"Because I'm watching your ass. In case you hadn't noticed, Skinner left an hour ago." Dec looks around the bar room confused.

"Oh yeah," he laughs. "Glad you got my back... plenty fuckers out there lined up to put a bullet through my skull," he says. "But with my boy back where he belongs, those Fallen-fucking-Saints... they can go fuck themselves."

Just hearing the name of the club that took Ryan's life makes me murderous.

Suddenly being back here, trying to get over that shit and expecting Beth to ever want me again, seems so far fucking fetched it's ridiculous.

That's until the bar door opens, and all the reasons I came back walks through it. She's dressed differently than she usually would be, I'm assuming that has something to do with Mia. The tight white lace dress she's wearing is far too short, and shows off way too much thigh to every fucker in here with a dick. Her tits are pushed tight together and she's wearing a long string of pearls that disappear into the tight gap between them, pearls that I want to take in my fist and use to drag her onto my lips.

Her hair is pinned up loosely, showing off her long slender neck, and she's wearing one of those tacky veils and tiara with *'bride to be'* written out of rhinestones.

She stops dead in her tracks when she sees me, and when our eyes fix, all the noise around us fades out and all I hear is my heartbeat thumping in my ears.

"I told you to keep him occupied," Mia comes at Dec, who gives her an intoxicated smile and shrugs.

"Asshole," Mia mutters.

"It's fine, we'll just sit over here," Beth steps forward and tugs at her friend's arm, I can tell she's a little tipsy by the clumsy way she moves. "We'll take a round of tequila over here," she calls over to the bartender as she drags a seething Mia over towards the empty booth at the back of the bar.

"Sorry man, I had no idea they'd be coming here," he apologizes, but I ain't listening, I'm too busy watching my girl. She's smiling and laughing with her friends and every now and then when her eyes flick over to me, I do nothing to hide the fact I'm watching her.

I want her to know that I'm not going anywhere. That I'm not giving up.

"We should go, man, I'll call the prospect to pick us up. We can leave the bikes in Stevie's lockup overnight," Dec slaps my chest.

"I ain't leaving," I shake my head, then nod at the barkeeper. I order and ask for another round of shots to be taken over to the girls, and then sink one myself before turning around and watching Beth's reaction.

When the tray full of tequilas gets placed on the table I watch her look up at the waitress in confusion, then her eyes meet with mine and she scowls at me. Mia's about to wade on over but Beth holds her back, whispering something in her ear before she picks up a shot and saunters her way across the bar floor towards me. The liquor intake has given her a little sass in her step, and I feel the smile tug on my lips when she stands in front of me, all confident and sexy as sin. Just like the girl I used to know.

"Thanks for the drinks," she says, her voice making all the hairs on my body prickle. "Thought I'd come over and share the toast." Her eyes peer over my shoulder, at the bar keeper, and within seconds he places a shot on the bar beside me. I humor her, lifting it up and waiting.

"Here's to me," she starts off so confidently. "For getting over the man who broke my heart." The smile slowly drains from her eyes, sliding from her cheeks, and her lips start to tremble. "For moving on and starting a fresh," she continues, tears magnify her pretty iris's, and I feel them stab at my heart like a blunt fucking knife.

"Here's to my future." The first tear drops on to her cheek and she quickly knocks back the shot before rushing away to the restroom.

Mia goes to chase after her but I block her path.

"I got this."

"The hell you have," she argues back. But Dec is on her, grabbing at his sister's waist and forcing her to sit on the stool bedside him.

"For once in your life do as you're fucking told and let my boy handle his business," he tells her, giving me a nod.

CHAPTER 5
BETH

"Beth let me in." His fist pounds heavy on the cubicle door. I should have known that even the ladies bathroom wouldn't be a safe place to hide from him. "You open this fuckin' door right now," he commands.

I snuffle back tears and use the back of my hands to wipe my cheeks. All the makeup Mia insisted I plaster on is probably half way down my face right now, and I rip the stupid veil out of my hair and chuck it at the floor.

"Beth Miller, you open this damn door or I'm crashing through it," Levi warns, and knowing that the man doesn't make empty threats, I reach forward and flick the lock.

Levi charges inside like a bull out the shoot, slamming the door shut behind him and making the whole cubicle rattle around us. He clicks the lock back across and just like yesterday in Marie's changing room, there's no escaping him.

He looks down to where I'm pathetically sitting on the toilet seat. And when I brave looking up at him through my lashes, I see all the pain I'm feeling reflecting back at me.

"Talk to me," he growls, his voice echoing in the small space surrounding us.

"You shouldn't have come back." I shake my head, feeling the onset of tears threatening again, and I can't let them break, if they do, they won't stop.

"I was happy, I was content with how my life was gonna be. And then..." The tears come streaming out, bringing with them a loud ugly sob. "It's cruel and it's selfish and it's too late," I manage to add.

Levi launches forward, his hands grabbing under my thighs and lifting me onto his body. I automatically cling to him as he crushes those strong arms around my middle, holding me tight against him. Our chests beat together fast, and comfort settles over me when I inhale the skin on his neck.

Nothing ever did come close to being held in Levi's arms.

I anchor his hips with my thighs and he turns, leaning me against the cubicle wall. One of his hands gripping the top of the divider while the other holds me by my waist.

And when he pulls his head back to look at me, his forehead is scrunched tight and his eyes are narrow.

It's intense and all too consuming, everything we once were, and I keep my arms tight around his neck, afraid to let him go again.

"I did this and I'm sorry," he starts, "But don't punish us both by marrying the wrong guy," he begs. I see how much he's hurting and I want to give into him, but years of hurting and forcing myself to get over him just can't allow me to.

"Promise me you won't do it. Give me time. Time to prove myself." His chest is rising and falling so fast. Levi Bridges is a badass. Me and this whole town know what he's capable of. He doesn't show weakness. And yet here he is, ripped at the seams.

I slowly shake my head, my heart shattering in my chest as I watch him swallow back disappointment, frustration forming in his eyes, as more tears drain out of mine.

We're so close, his body so tight to mine that I feel his hard cock pressing at the space between my legs, and suddenly I hunger for him in a way I've trained myself to forget.

"Let me fix this for us," he rasps, keeping me pinned to the cubicle wall with his body and the arm that's stretched above my head. The thumb of his other hand softly brushing the wet tears from my cheek before he cups my chin and lifts up my head. He focuses all his attention on my mouth, wetting his lips by rubbing them together.

"Don't," I whisper weakly, my legs trembling around his hips.

But Levi shows no mercy, crashing his mouth onto mine and reminding me of everything he snatched away from me. It doesn't matter how much I want to hate him or how hard I try to fight it. I can't stop myself from sinking into the comfort it gives me.

For a few brief seconds everything feels right again, the tension in our bodies subsides, and the arch of his hand squeezes at my jaw making it impossible for me to escape him.

I ache to feel him inside me again, and he must sense it when his hand fumbles to loosen his belt and his fingers brush over the lace barrier between us. Rough skin connects with my sensitive flesh when he slips my panties to the side. Just as his knees dip to push that thick heavy cock I'm craving inside me, I somehow find the energy to push at his strong chest and force him off my lips.

"Stop." I close my eyes, because I can't let this happen, no matter how much I want it. I can't cheat on Laurie.

Levi shakes his head, moving in to kiss me again but I hold firm.

"No," I tell him sternly, feeling his body sag with disappointment, his bicep tenses tight as his hand grips at the cubicle screen above my head like he might rip it apart.

"You're too late, I'm marrying Laurie."

Levi's forehead drops onto mine, his eyes penetrating all the hurt he's feeling so deep into my soul that I feel my bones shudder. And when his hand slowly moves back up my body, I allow myself the pleasure of its touch for what I know has to be the last time.

The heat in his fingertips burn at my skin as they clasp my jaw again, forcing me to stare right back at him.

"You go ahead and do that if you think it will make you feel better. But we both know a ring on your finger and a piece of paper ain't never gonna make you his." He grips at me tighter, his nostrils flaring.

"Run on back to your fiancé, Beth, play house, bake him pies and fake him smiles. But when he's inside you…" Levi purposely ensures the thick tip of his cock slides between my pussy lips, and my hips automatically roll to seek out more, "…Don't ever pretend to yourself you ain't wishing it was me."

His lips push hard onto mine and his cock applies just the right pressure to sustain the throb in my clit, just for a few blissful seconds. Then everything comes crashing down when he reaches both his hands behind his neck, taking hold of my wrists and dragging my arms away. He lets my feet drop back to the floor before he takes a step back. And the space he puts between us while he rearranges his jeans feels cold and empty.

I wonder if he knows that I'm suffering every ounce of the pain he is when those cold eyes, full of hurt glance me over. Or, if when he clicks the lock open and storms back out to the bar, that he's left my poor heart crushed all over again.

CHAPTER 6
LEVI

"I heard you were back in town." Pops stares across the table at me, his eyes fixed and unforgiving, while Momma fusses around the kitchen insisting on fixing me something to eat. I never told them I was back in town and I know that will have hurt Momma. But the truth is, I've been avoiding Pops.

He retired after his road accident, but he'll always be a Dirty Soul at heart, and I know how disappointed he was in me when I left town. Disappointed enough to not have spoken to me the whole time I've been away.

"Good news travels fast." I put on a brave smile for Mom who smiles back warmly. She never was a typical old lady. She's more the nurturing, homely type. I really don't know how she ended up with Pops but it's clear how much she loves him.

Though, I always had a hunch that she wanted me to take a different path to him. Yet here I am cut and all. Walking in my father's footsteps and still not giving him anything to be proud about.

"You back for good, boy?" he asks.

"Depends," I shrug.

"You came back because you heard about Beth." Mom's hand rests on my shoulder as she places the peanut butter and jelly sandwich in front of me.

"Shoulda known it'd be pussy gotcha back here before

loyalty to your brothers," Pops quips, his words stinging exactly how he intends them to.

"You could have told me about Beth," I look up at Mom. Me and her speak on the phone every Sunday, she never once mentioned Beth being with anyone else.

"I didn't think you'd wanna hear it. She invited us to the wedding," she tries to sound enthusiastic, but her sad expression lets her down.

"You goin'?" I clear my throat and take a bite out the sandwich, suddenly feeling like a kid again.

"You two were together a long time. A lot of happy memories I have include her," she says fondly. "I'd like to see her on her wedding day."

I nod back so she knows I understand.

"Lucky escape if you ask me," Pops takes another opportunity to slice into me. "That girl deserves to marry a man. Not someone who runs at the first sign of trouble." And that just about fucking does it.

"I lost my best friend," my fist comes down hard on the table. I don't wanna upset Momma but what am I expected to do when he keeps on chipping away at me. The old man don't flinch, his eyes remaining cold and focused on mine.

"I had to watch him die in my arms, knowing I couldn't save him." I try to keep a lid on my rage for Mom's sake, all while holding back all the angry tears I don't want Pops to see.

"I made those fuckers pay for what they did to him, but no matter how hard I tried I couldn't see any justice. So, if you wanna make me feel like shit Pops, you're wasting your time. I already hit rock bottom and now I'm fuckin' trapped down there. There ain't redemption for me, not while I'm my own judge."

He stares back, his expression not changing and when I feel Momma's hand stroke through my hair, I quickly remind myself to cool off. She hasn't seen me in so long, I don't want this visit to end bad.

"What happened to Ryan wasn't your fault," she assures me. I don't have to look up at her to know her eyes will be full of tears. Ryan was like a second son to her, he moved in here when he was fifteen after his Momma ran off with a traveler. His father was always drinking and whoring at the club, so Momma naturally took care of him. She raised him up from an angry abandoned teenager into the level headed man he became.

"Sweetheart, I know you're hurting about Beth. You and her had something really special. But you can't ruin her day for her. She moved on. She deserves to be happy."

"I gotta get back to the club."

I can't be here no more, hearing her sympathy while feeling my old man's disappointment is too much, so I stand up from the table and hug Mom.

"Promise you'll say goodbye before you leave again," she whispers. She knows I'm too late to fix this, that Beth is gonna marry Laurie and that there ain't no way I'll be able to stick around and watch another man give her the life I should have.

"Promise," I tell her, nodding my head at Dad before I make my way out the back door towards my bike and kick my wheel hard with my boot outta pure frustration.

I keep letting people down. Momma feels sorry for me, Pops is ashamed of me. I'm nowhere close to being the person I thought I'd be. The Levi Bridges who left town all those years ago was a shell.

I'm still a fucking shell. I got no purpose, no hope. Only regrets.

Jumping on my bike I kickstart the engine and ride on, because it's time to face the person I've really been avoiding since I've been back in town.

As I'm walking towards his grave, I can't help remembering the day we buried him. How cruel and cold I was to Beth, she was trying to comfort me in that beautiful soft way that comes so effortlessly to her, and all I did was push her away.

Anger was festering inside me, guilt infecting me like a poison. She tried to be there for me, then when I rejected all that affection she understood and tried giving me space.

Nothing was bringing him back though.

I reach his spot and stare at his grave. I can't block out the sick visions of how he'll look down there now, they taint all the good memories I got of my best friend.

There's a single white rose lying over his tombstone, and I wonder if it was Beth that put it there.

Her and Ryan were always close, back when we lost him I never considered the pain she'd be feeling too. I was far too caught up in self-loathing. Beth would still think about him like I do. Maybe me being back in town brought her here to him. She always did go to him for advice.

Not that the fucker knew Jack shit about relationships. Ryan never had a girl, not one he cared about the way I did Beth. I guess that's just another thing in life that he missed out on.

I pick up the rose, my rough hands sliding over the velvety petals. Pure, white and soft. I breathe them in through my nose and the crisp, fresh scent reminds me of her.

"Would you let her go?" I ask him, knowing that even if he could hear me, he can't give me a fuckin' answer.

Though I can make a damn good guess at what it would be.

He'd tell me to fight.

Well, at least that's what he'd say to the old me. Ryan wouldn't recognize the man standing in front of him now.

Weak, cursed and fucking lonely.

I close my eyes and remember that night, my hands covered in his blood, the scared look in his eyes when he figured that I wasn't gonna be able to save him.

He spent those last few seconds of his life gripping my hand like a helpless child, and it's damn hard to get a vision like that out ya head.

I shake myself back to the present and place the rose back

where it was, then I wipe away the stray tear that I let fall for my friend.

"Sorry," I whisper. One single word, that seems so small and insignificant for the price he paid for my mistake.

Ryan should be here, me, him and Dec should be running this town together like we always planned. I fucked it all up.

I head back to my bike and ride into town, parking up on the opposite side of the street to the coffee shop where Beth still works. I watch her through the glass, serving customers and smiling in that beautiful, effortless way of hers.

I don't know how long I lean against the lamppost and watch her for, but the air turns colder and the daylight fades. Then when a smart looking car pulls up outside, I watch Laurie Preston get out the driver's seat and stroll inside.

He's got that spring in his step that comes with absolute contentment. They come out together a few minutes later, his arms draped over her shoulder as she locks up, and watching them feels like taking a long, jagged dagger to the heart.

Kills me to admit it, but they look good together. They look happy. Maybe I've been reading Beth all wrong. Maybe Laurie is exactly what she needs in her life.

He opens the door for her, kissing her cheek before she ducks inside. And my body suddenly feels too heavy for my legs to hold. My time's running out, my fight starting to fade, and I feel her slipping further and further away.

I wait until they pull off before moving on myself, heading for the club and hoping I can drown myself in enough liquor to numb out all my feelings.

The club is busy so I sit at the corner of the bar. I must give off the impression that I want to be alone because no one bothers me. And it's there that I wait until I've drunk and smoked enough shit for all the thoughts in my head to start making sense.

Hours have passed, and the liquor ain't working, so I pick up the phone and dial her number, hoping it's still the same one and I get to hear her voice again.

"Hello," she answers with a soft whisper. It's late now, and being the night before her wedding day I'll bet she's getting herself an early night.

"Hello?" her voice whispers again, speaking right to my soul and piercing me with pain.

"Be happy, Beth," my voice cracks, and I swallow back all the other words I got for her. This is what she really needs to hear.

I have to let her go.

I don't give her the chance to respond before hanging up the phone, launching it at the wall and nodding to Helen for another bottle.

CHAPTER 7
BETH

"You know if your Momma could see you now she'd be bawling her eyes out," Mia tells me when I come out the bathroom and stand in front of her and Annie.

"She's right, Momma would be so proud of you." Annie snuffles back her tears.

"Jesus. Don't go crying, your daddy will notice you're wearing mascara," Mia warns her, quickly ripping a tissue from the box on the vanity unit and passing it over.

"You don't think he'll show up today, do you?" I press my hand against my stomach attempting to suppress the nerves.

"Dec's gonna sit at the back of the chapel, and I got Skinner on duty back at the club. Levi ain't leaving the clubhouse," Mia assures me.

I close my eyes and take a breath, I can't stop remembering that deep husk in his tone when he called last night. It felt like he was saying goodbye, like I'd lost him all over again, and it hurt like hell.

"Come on, you're not gonna think about him today. Today you become Mrs. Preston and the whole town is gonna be talking about how beautiful you look." Mia stands up and takes my hand in hers. "You really do look beautiful. And I ain't even bullshittin' like I did when you wore that awful two-piece to senior prom."

The door knocks, interrupting our giggles and my heart leaps into my throat as it opens, though it quickly settles back into place when it's my father who steps inside.

"You look incredible." He places a kiss on my cheek. "We better not keep your husband waiting. He might change his mind and let me keep you," he smiles, hooking his arm for me to take. Annie passes my bouquet and offers me an encouraging smile. Before her and Mia lead us out the door towards the car.

Father doesn't talk for the whole journey, I wonder if he's thinking about Momma, wishing that she was here like I am. Maybe he's thinking back to the day he married her in the same little chapel I'm about to give my vows to Laurie in.

Mom and Dad were a happy couple, he hasn't been the same since we lost her, and I really hope he finds that happiness again.

He squeezes my hand when we arrive outside the chapel and as I get out of the car, I find myself searching for signs of Levi. I'm not sure if I'm relieved or disappointed when the only bike I see is Declan's.

I look at the chapel in front of me, my chest starting to tighten and my hands trembling. Today is a new beginning, I should be excited. So why does this feel like an end.

I spent so long praying for Levi to come back to me, years, refusing to believe that a love like ours could be over.

I thought that getting with Laurie would heal my heart.

But Levi being back, the way it felt to have him touch me again, has made me realize that I never healed. I just forgot.

And just like that, I feel void again, on the day I'm supposed to be getting married. When my heart should be bursting with love and joy, it feels shrunk and empty.

"Come on, sweetheart." Father guides me closer to the chapel door, while Mia and Annie take their first steps inside. The organ starts to play and I suck in the fresh air through my nostrils, taking one more glance over my shoulder to check for Levi. Father moves us forward onto the thick red carpet that's lining the aisle, and all heads turn towards me. Their happy smiles, full of well wishes and congratulations making me feel like a fraud.

I flick my eyes to the left and spot Dec, he's even made an effort and put a shirt and tie on under his cut. He nods at me reassuringly as I pass him.

Levi's parents are here too, fifth row from the front, and I watch Carol dab the corner of her eye with a tissue. She knows, like I do, that it should be her son waiting for me at the top of this altar, and as I take each step closer towards Laurie, I feel the ache in my chest spread a little wider.

When we get to the priest, Mia takes my bouquet and I turn to face him. The man who is gonna be my husband, who will father my children and share all my future memories. Good or bad, rich or poor. Through sickness and health.

I will be his.

He smiles at me so warmly, and I force a smile past the tears in my eyes to replicate it before pulling my gaze from his and looking back down the aisle. The door is still open, the town outside empty and quiet. There's no sign of Levi, and I realize that's what's hurting so bad.

It's what's been hurting since he told me to be happy.

Because how am I supposed to be happy without him. I turn my head back to Laurie and reach out my hand to stroke over the dimple on his right cheek. I'm not being fair to him. Laurie is a good person, he deserves to own a woman's heart and he will never own mine.

"I'm so sorry," I whisper, then ignoring the gasps and chaos that breaks out around me, I pick up the front of my dress and I run.

CHAPTER 8
LEVI

"Stop lookin' at that clock," Skinner tells me. Him and Jay are trying to distract me by packing up the guns that Jimmer and the boys from Colorado will be picking up tomorrow. We got a Prospect guarding the door and I don't know if it's to keep watch, or extra security to try and keep me in. Either way, I focus on the job I'm doing checking each unit and making it secure for the journey on to Nevada.

I ain't said anything to Dec yet but I'm thinking about joining them on the road, I need to get out of this town.

"It'll all be over now anyway," I shrug stubbing my smoke out in the ashtray and making my way to the bar to pour myself something strong.

Skinner looks back at me almost sympathetically. It surprises me, I didn't know the fucker was capable of emotion.

"Thanks for babysitting," I toast the shot of vodka in my hand at him sarcastically. "There was really no need. I wouldn't have fucked today up for her. Beth belongs with Laurie Preston. She'll move into his fancy fucking house and I'll bet they're already working on making them beautiful kids that should have been mine too." I laugh cruelly, knocking it back and slamming the glass on the bar.

"There'll be other women, hell man, there's plenty of 'em around here."

"Spoken like a man who ain't had every other fucking woman ruined for him." I point my finger at him before pouring myself another.

"Never again," I shake my head. "Levi Bridges ain't gonna feel shit from now on. I'm gonna keep riding nomad, and only worry about myself."

Skinner shrugs and takes a seat beside me at the bar.

"What would you have done if I'd have tried to leave?" I ask, the guy's built like a fucking grizzly, he's a few years older than me and Dec and one of the most valuable members of this club. But Skinner was never made to be a leader, he's all braun and no fucking brains.

"I got told to shoot before I let you out that door," he laughs back at me.

"Mia?" I guess.

"Yep," he chuckles, starting to roll a blunt now that he's officially off duty.

I lean forward and rest my elbows on the bar, trying not to think about what she'll be doing now. It's pointless checking my phone again. I've done it so many times this morning. Waiting and hoping for that text to come through and ask me to go to her. But it's too late for that now.

Both me and Skinner jump into defense mode when the club doors barge open, relaxing when it's Mia who storms past the prospect and heads straight for me.

I can't help smirking at how ridiculous she looks in the long flouncy dress she's wearing. Even if her eyes are seething into mine with the venom of a thousand cobras. She rips the delicate lace gloves off her hands, then snatches the bottle out of mine.

"You gonna tell him, or should I?" she rages at her brother before knocking back a mouthful, and I watch a huge cocky smile rise on my friend's face.

"I'm surprised to see ya here," he says, casually taking a stool.

"Where else would I fucking be? Your sister..."

"Nah, brother. I mean I'm surprised you ain't with your girl... since she just ran out on her wedding."

I swear my heart stops beating as I let his words sink in.

"Wait, are you telling me she didn't marry him?" I check I got this right. Hope can do fucked up things to a man's head.

"She sprinted from that chapel like the flames of Satan were dancin' at her feet." Dec grins back.

"Holy fuck. I gotta go find her."

I go to move but Mia blocks my way.

"No, you fucked with her head enough already. She knows where to find you. If she wants to see you, she'll come to you. I'm gonna go looking for her. Skinner, if he tries to walk out that door you shoot him in the back of his head," she commands.

"You can't expect me to just sit here waiting around," I shout across the room as she storms back towards the door, but Dec shakes his head at me. "Sis is right on this one. Girl just ran out on her wedding. The fact she ain't here says she needs to clear her head. Give her some space and just be grateful that your girl saw sense. She'll come for you, Levi, just let her do it on her own terms."

CHAPTER 9
BETH

I had no idea when I started running that I would end up here. Or that sitting on my knees in front of Ryan's grave on the day I should be getting married would bring me the comfort I need.

Growing up, I was the eldest of my siblings, always the one everyone depended on. Ryan had been like a big brother to me.

I press my hand over his name wishing he was still here. Someone else must have been here recently, there's a fresh rose placed on his headstone. Perhaps his mother finally grew a conscience and decided to visit, or maybe Levi left it for him. Whoever it was, I'm grateful Ryan isn't lonely out here, he always did like to have people around him.

I visit as often as I can. Talking to Ryan always used to be so easy. The fact he was the strong silent type, makes him not talking back now not seem as strange. Usually, I tell him about what's been happening lately, or I talk about old times and how much I miss him and Momma, but today all I can do is snuffle back tears.

The clouds slowly cast a dark shadow over us, and when the rain starts to fall I choose to remain with him rather than run for shelter. I torture myself, imaging how things might have been if I hadn't been so damn selfish the night we lost him.

"I wish you were still here. You always understood what was

going on in his head," I speak to the granite stone, the rain's coming down hard now and disguising my tears.

"How am I supposed to forget that he left me here to grieve you alone? I didn't marry Laurie today, but I still don't know if I'm ready to forgive five years of hurt."

The wet grass stains my dress and when I wipe my eyes, black tears streak my fingers.

"I'm sorry this happened to you," I sob, "And I'm sorry that I don't know if I can forgive him for running out on me. If you were here, that's what you'd tell me I should do, right?" I feel like I'm fighting for my next breath, my skin shivering from the chill of the rain and I wish I could hear him tell me everything is going to be okay.

"I really thought Levi hated me for what happened. We were never the same after, and I know he left because he blamed me," my breath hitches as I speak through my tears. "He tried but he just couldn't forgive me being the reason you weren't here anymore. I don't see how that's changed."

Everyone thinks Levi left town because he couldn't get past what happened to his friend, but I knew the real truth. He just couldn't bear to be around the reason he lost him.

"I'm heading out," Ryan pokes his head around the door to tell us.

"Where ya headin'?" Levi asks, me and him are laid out together on his bed watching some lame assed film that neither of us are really into.

"The club of course, you guys up for a few? Some of the Long Beach boys are visiting and I'll bet they brought with 'em some of that good Mexican shit," Ryan wiggles his eyebrows trying to tempt us.

"Nah, we're having an easy one tonight." Levi shakes his

head and I know it's because I've just moaned to him for over an hour about how bad things are at home.

Since Momma went back into nursing, all the chores at home have fallen on me. It feels good to have a night off from helping with kids' homework and breaking up fights.

"Suit ya selves," Ryan shrugs, backing out the door and leaving us alone.

"We could have gone if you wanted," I tell Levi, though I'm glad we haven't. It's rare for the two of us to get any time to ourselves. Daddy isn't exactly welcoming to Levi so we spend most of our time either here or hanging out at the club.

The Dirty Soul clubhouse isn't the usual place a girl like me would hang out, but I'm Mia Turner's best friend, her daddy's the Prez of the club, and her brother is built like a mountain.

No one is gonna mess with me. Especially now that everyone knows I'm Levi Bridges' girl too.

It gets late, Levi's pops is probably spending the night at the club, we've just heard his Mom go to bed and we're halfway through watching our second lame film of the night.

"This sucks." Levi shifts on to his side, propping himself up on his elbow. "You want me to make you come instead?" he asks as his hand slowly slides into the front of my jeans. I suck air when his finger softly skims through my pussy lips and when he hits that sweet spot, there's no way I could refuse him, not even if I wanted to.

I lean forward to kiss him, but he pulls his head away from me.

"Nah-Ah. you look too fucking pretty when you come. I wanna watch this one…" he rubs his lips together, "…then taste the next one." His eyes lower to where his hand is rubbing me and all I can do is nod my agreement as I sink into his touch.

"Shit," he curses, suddenly pulling away when his phone starts to vibrate on the nightstand, but I grab his forearm and hold him firm.

"Leave it, it won't hurt just this once. Please?" I beg breathlessly. It'll be someone from the club. Being at each other's beckon call is all part of being a member and Levi takes that responsibility very seriously.

But I'm too close.

Levi keeps working me, stretching his neck to check who it is.

"It's Ryan," he looks back at me apologetically.

"I don't give a shit if it's the President," I moan, pushing myself tighter against his fingers and feeling that rush of pleasure start to climb higher in the base of my stomach. "You made me a promise, Levi Bridges."

CHAPTER 10
LEVI

"You made me a promise, Levi Bridges." The smile on her face is too fucking wicked to refuse. So I leave the phone to ring out while I watch my girl come for me. Once is never enough, and after Beth soaks my fingers, I rip the jeans off her and toss them out of my way.

Fucking Ryan, he's probably high and needs a ride home, that or he's calling to tell me to stop being pussy struck and go hangout with him and the boys.

But Ryan ain't the one that's got my dick hard right now, and as I push Beth's thighs apart and sink my head between them, the long, satisfied moan she makes when I slide my tongue through her pretty little pussy assures me I made the right decision in staying home tonight.

Beth is stressed out at home, she hates her job and right now I wanna be all the satisfaction she needs. I take my sweet time with her, making love to her perfect body and kissing every inch of her skin. Then I hold her tight to me for way after we're done.

"You better see what Ryan wanted, he prob wants a ride," she whispers eventually, and I kiss her forehead and get out of bed, tossing over her jeans and grabbing my phone from where it's fallen on to the floor.

"I got eleven missed calls," I roll my eyes, pulling on my own jeans after checking my phone. "And he's left me a voicemail."

Beth smiles back at me lazily. "We'll go pick him up together, I'm suddenly feeling hungry." She stretches her body out like a lazy cat while I dial my voicemail. Something in my gut is telling me that something's wrong. Ryan doesn't leave voicemails.

"Levi," Ryan's voice whispers, sounding on edge. "I'm outside The Casket and I need you to get here pronto. Don't ask questions just fucking get here." The phone goes dead and I feel a chill shudder my bones.

"Ryan's at The Casket he wants me to go to him," I tell Beth.

"The Casket?" She sits up looking worried. "Isn't that a Fallen Saints hangout?"

"Yeah, and he left me that voicemail half an hour ago."

This is bad, really fucking bad.

"I gotta go get him." I rush to get what I need.

"No," Beth scurries off the bed and grabs hold of my arm.

"You aren't going there on your own. It's too dangerous. And what the hell is Ryan doing there anyway?"

She's right, none of this makes any sense.

"I have no idea, but I need to get to him." I pull away from her to grab a T-shirt and my cut.

"Please don't go alone, Levi, I'm begging you," she pleads, her pretty eyes suddenly panicked and brimming with tears.

I should have answered my damn phone on his first call, talked him out of whatever the fuck he's caught up in. But it's too late now and Beth's right, walking on to Fallen Saints territory alone is suicide.

"I'll go to the club first and round up a few of the guys. I won't go alone," I promise her.

"I'm coming too." Beth quickly gathers the rest of her clothes.

"You can come, but you stay at the club until I get back," I warn.

"Whatever you say, let's just get going," she agrees.

I ride to the club as fast as I can with Beth clinging on tight behind me, what the fuck is Ryan thinking going there alone?

The club is in full party mode when I park up outside and I grab Beth's hand and lead her through the door.

"Go find Mia," I kiss her hard on the lips, leaving her to find her best friend while I rally up some support. If we're going to The Casket, we're going in numbers.

My Prez, Dec's old man, is over in the corner with Davey, the Long Beach Charter's President and that's where I head first.

"Is Ryan here?" I ask, hoping to fucking god that he's backed out of whatever it was he was doing.

"Nah he stormed outta here a while ago," Prez answers.

And both the old men's faces hold the same confusion and worry when I explain why I'm looking for him.

"Take, Skinner, Dec and Zander," Prez tells me.

"Brax rode in with me and my boys, best take him too, he's a handy mother fucker, wetting some Saints might loosen him up a bit," Davey adds.

I nod at them both, before going in search of Dec.

He doesn't ask questions when I interrupt the convo he's having with one of the club whores, and quickly rushes off to gather the others while I get us some arsenal.

We always carry, but I raid the stockroom out back and pick up a few extras for everyone.

I find Brax, the nomad who road in with the others, sitting by himself at the bar, he's a mean looking fucker and he shakes his head when I offer him an AK. When he pulls open his cut revealing a double holster and the impressive sized knife attached to his belt, he proves he's good to go.

"Be careful," Beth stops me before I can make it to the door.

"Always," I promise, kissing my girl's lips and feeling the adrenaline start to pump.

When I step outside, the cold air bites at my skin and suddenly everything around me turns to chaos.

A blacked-out van speeds towards us, gunshots are fired and I check over my shoulder that Beth's still inside before I grab at Dec and drag him with me onto the ground.

The van skids to a halt in front of us and more shots get let off as the side door opens, a limp body gets tossed onto the road. I manage to shoot a few off myself as I scramble on my knees, keeping low and moving towards the body.

I don't need to check to know that it's him, my instincts tell me everything as the van screeches off. And when I finally reach my best friend, I'm sickened by the damage they've done to him.

His face is beaten, unrecognizable, and there's a growing puddle of blood on the tarmac beneath him, I shift his body to try and find where it's coming from. Dec's screaming some shit in my ear, bikes are revving and heading off in pursuit, but all I can focus on is trying to stop my friend from bleeding out. I manage to find the injury, a huge gash to his stomach, and when I press my hand over it to try and make it stop, blood flows through my fingers.

"Ryan, we're getting help," I assure him, he's trying to breathe but he's panicking and I have to forget how fucking scared I am and be strong for him.

My fingers are slippery and sticky with blood, but I take his hand in mine and I hold it firm. I don't know how many times I tell him it's gonna be okay and I don't know which one of us stops believing it first. But even when blankness replaces the fear on his face and his body stops trembling, I can still hear myself saying the words.

"Levi," Dec's voice shakes me back to the present and when I focus my attention on him, his eyes direct me in a different direction.

Beth's standing in the doorway to the bar, her white dress stained with dirt and soaked to her body.

She came, and suddenly I don't know what to say to her.

"Thank God you're okay," Mia comes rushing out of nowhere, hugging her best friend so tight she nearly knocks Beth off balance. "Get this girl a drink, something strong. Christ babe, you're freezing."

Beth blanks out everything Mia's saying, her eyes set on mine as she steps closer to me.

Her chest is rising heavily, and the goosebumps that have popped up under her skin are glistening with rain.

She looks like such a beautiful tragedy, I wanna wrap her up in my arms and never let her go.

"I need to talk to you," she says, ignoring the fact that everyone in the club is staring at us.

"You wanna go upstairs?" I stand up from my stool and reach out for her hand, and automatically she takes it in hers. Then, she thinks twice and quickly snatches it away from me again.

"Yeah," she nods, trying to keep a brave face.

All the rooms here are pretty basic, they weren't really designed to be lived in, and as I open the door into my room I suddenly wish we were having this conversation somewhere else.

"Take a seat." I clear the chair in the corner of my clothes for her but she shakes her head in refusal.

"I'd rather stand" she tells me, already starting to pace the floor. I nod back, sinking into the chair myself and deciding to let her take the lead on this.

"Why did you come back?" she snaps her head up at me after making a few laps across the floor.

"I told you why. To stop you from marrying a guy you didn't love."

"How did you know I didn't love him, Levi, what did you think turning back up in town after all this time was gonna achieve?" she shakes her head like she's struggling to understand.

"Looks like I got what I wanted," I smirk, trying to lighten her mood. But she ain't having it.

"This isn't a joke. You can't just walk into my life again and expect things to go back to how they were. I'm a different person now. You're a different person. Jesus fucking Christ, Levi, I was trying to be happy and you came back and fucked it all up." She breaks into tears, tears that make me want to hurt myself for being the one who caused them.

"I'm sorry." I stand up and move to comfort her.

But she holds out her hand as a barrier between us, "Don't touch me, I can't think straight when you touch me and I need to get all this out."

I take a step back, despite feeling wounded. If my girl wants space, she's got it.

"Why?" She shakes her head looking distraught. "You left me here to grieve Ryan, thinking that you hated me. I lost my mom, you never came back for me when I needed you. Then just as I'm about to start a future, you show your face again. You had every right to blame me for what happened to Ryan, Levi, and I'm so fucking sorry. I hurt every day because of it. But I didn't deserve to be abandoned."

"What?" I stare back at her in shock. "How was what happened to Ryan your fault? I left because I blamed myself. And I came back because I love you. I've loved you every day since I left. I've been empty inside without you."

"Then why didn't you come back sooner? Why leave me to suffer? Levi, I felt like I was fucking drowning in this town, everywhere I looked there was a memory of us. You were the only good thing I had, and you left me without an explanation. You tore out my heart and took it with you and now you…" her sobs get the better of her and she has to take a breath. "…I can't do this." She starts to head for the door, but I can't let her leave, not until this is resolved. So I bolt after her, managing to catch up and slam my hand into the door above her head before she can open it.

I feel her whimpers, my body so tight to hers that her heartbeat thuds through her back against my chest, and I realize that nothing I can say is gonna be enough to explain how sorry I am.

I need to make her feel it.

Reaching my arm around her body, I hold her firm. My lips moving forward and brushing over her neck. Beth remains still, her body shivering from the soaked dress she's wearing.

"Take this dress off," I slide my hand over her thigh and grasp the silky fabric between my fingers. It ain't just the fact it's making her cold. it's the fact she chose this dress for him that makes me want to rip it off her body and set fucking fire to the damn thing.

I hitch the dress higher up her thigh until I feel her flesh on my fingertips, then I pull my body from hers so I can rip open the ribbons holding her bodice in place.

"Levi," she breathes my name, but I keep on ripping at the ribbon.

"I want you out of this fucking dress, Beth." I stay focused, and she eventually gives in and helps me tear the thing from her body.

She turns to face me, revealing the pretty white lace she's been wearing underneath it. The perfect underwear for a groom to devour his bride in, and I make no time to admire how incredible she looks before I unhook the bra and rid her of it.

I'm too desperate to touch her again to be gentle, and squeeze one of her perfect round tits in my fist as my teeth clamp around the nipple of her other one.

Beth's body sags, either from relief or defeat, despite all the hate she's got for me right now she's finally giving in to her body's desires.

Lifting her off the ground I press her tight against the door, moving my lips to her mouth and taking back everything I should never have let go.

Beth kisses me back with the same hunger. Our bodies have been apart for far too long.

We both have a lot to talk about. I've got a lot of apologies to make, but right now this is what we need.

"Fuck me, Levi." Her fingernails dig in to my shoulders through my T-shirt and knowing that I can't deny my girl a damn thing, I give her exactly what she wants, carrying her over to the bed.

I lie her on the mattress, and she wipes her tears and smiles up at me as I pull the shirt off my back and pull down my jeans. My cock is rock solid, desperate to be inside her again, but I got to be considerate.

"You need me to rubber up?" I check, Beth was on the pill when I left town. I've worn a condom with every girl I've ever been with since her so I know I'm clean.

She shakes her head back at me, before her eyes lower onto my cock. And the way she licks those lips of hers has me fucking leaking already.

I've thought for a long time about how things would be if ever I got the chance to be with her like this again, each time in my head I'd worshipped her, taken my time to enjoy every sweet inch of her again. But all the tension inside me ain't gonna allow that to happen. I need to be inside her, to make her mine again, and so I move forward into the space she makes for me between her legs.

My cock finds its way to her entrance, and her warm, wet pussy soaks my tip as I edge inside her. I want to savor it, to feel her tight pussy take every inch of me, but possessiveness prevails and she gets me in one hard thrust that seems to smooth over every fucking scrape Beth Miller ever carved to my heart.

"Jesus!" Her back arches off the mattress and I hold steady

inside her. I can't think about her being with him, the thought makes me so angry that I'd fuck her black and blue. Instead, I focus on the fact that she's mine again, and that as long as I'm drawing breath there will never be another man for her.

"You've always been mine. I won't let you go again," I remind her, starting to move slowly, pulling out and pushing back in, my hands gripping at her skin like they've been starved of her contact. Our lips fuse together and there's nothing I can think of that tops the feeling of owning her again.

I thrust my hips into hers, hard but slow, her tight walls squeezing around me while she grips at the sheets and pants into my mouth.

"I'm gonna come, Levi," she warns. Her body fidgeting underneath mine, and her fingers scratching at my back.

"Not yet, baby. Together." I can feel myself edging closer, so I grab at her thigh and hold her leg over my shoulder, my fingers indenting her flesh as I fuck my cock hard and fast into her.

"I… holy fuck I'm gonna…"

"Go," I tell her, feeling myself brimming, "Give it to me. Just like you used to, soak my fucking cock, Beth." I hold her eyes with mine and watch the pleasure spread over her face as she comes apart, her pussy tightening around me and drawing everything out of me. And for those few seconds, nothing else matters. The pain I've caused, the people we've lost. It's just me and her, reunited. Together as we always should have been. And when my cock stops throbbing to the beat of her pulse, I let her leg fall onto the mattress and my body flop on top of hers.

"I fucking missed us," I whisper breathlessly.

CHAPTER 11
BETH

"Take it you two sorted out your differences?" Mia is waiting for me downstairs when I sneak through the bar. I left Levi sleeping, I'll deal with him later, right now I need to get cleaned up and face what happened yesterday.

"We didn't really get to talk," I admit awkwardly, taking the coffee she offers me.

"You owe Laurie answers," she tells me, and I quickly add guilt to the long list of emotions that are swirling around my head.

"I couldn't marry him, Mia, I didn't love him, I never have. It's always been Levi."

"So why are you sneaking out the back door?" she looks back at me judgingly.

"I need space. I've got to think about what I do now. Levi left town for a reason, who's to say he won't run scared again, and my heart can't lose him a second time. I need answers and it just seems like when we're together all that we want to do is…"

"Get to fucking?" Mia interrupts me with a huge smile on her face. "Here," she hands me a set of keys. "I spoke to your dad last night and told him you were staying at mine to get your head straight. Go back to mine, take a shower and some time to think about what you want. The place is empty. Dad's on a fishing trip and Dec stayed here last night with one of the whores."

"Love you." I lean forward and kiss my friend's cheek.

"Ewww, get those lips off me, I don't want anything that's touched Levi Bridges cock near my face."

"How was Dad when you spoke to him?" I change the subject, feeling awful for the embarrassment I must have caused him. I was so wrapped up in myself last night I didn't even think about how angry he's gonna be.

"He's... well, he's your dad," she shrugs helplessly, "Maybe call him when you've had a shower."

I pass her back the coffee. I haven't got time to finish it.

"I'm gonna message Reena and ask if I can work today. I need to do something normal," I tell her, knowing she'll argue.

"You're crazy, Beth, the whole town will be talking about what happened." Mia, as expected, looks back at me like I've lost my mind.

"I know and I'd rather face them head on and get it over with. I'll call Laurie, and Dad but then I'm going to work," I tell her firmly.

"And when you gonna talk to Levi?" she questions, and I don't answer that question, just quickly make my way out the door, get in her car and drive off, hoping I can start thinking straight.

CHAPTER 12

LEVI

When I wake up to an empty space beside me, I wonder if I dreamt up last night, until I see her dress still on the floor and realize it was real. There ain't no sign of her though.

Me and Beth spent last night making up for all the years we've been apart. It was perfect. And I'm pissed that she's left without giving me the chance to talk to her.

I quickly throw on some clothes, grab my cell and go looking for her.

When I check the time, it's way past lunchtime and I can't remember a time when I've slept in so late. The satisfaction of having her back beside me again obviously had me resting too fucking easily.

I rush down the stairs, through the bar, ready to get on my bike and go looking for her.

"If you're looking for the runaway bride, she left a few hours ago," Mia's voice stops me. She's sitting on one of the leather couches at the back of the bar, flicking through her phone.

"Where is she?"

"She went to get a shower, then she went to work." Even Mia seems surprised to be telling me that part.

"She went to work? She can't have had a shift, ain't she supposed to be on her honeymoon or some shit?"

"She asked to go in. Apparently she wanted normality," Mia shrugs.

"I'm gonna go find her." I turn to walk out but Mia calls me back.

"You need to tell me why you left town. Beth's my best friend and for me to be okay about this, I need to know why you hurt her."

I feel my shoulders sag as I turn back to face her. Mia's a pain in the ass but I can't help but love her for the way she protects Beth. She deserves answers too, and I'm gonna have to get used to opening up if I'm gonna convince Beth to trust me again.

I sit on the couch opposite and lean forward, resting my arms on my knees.

"The night Ryan went to the clubhouse. The night they…" I can't even say the fucking words. "He called me and I ignored the call. Beth was having a tough time and I wanted to be there for her so I let the phone ring out." For once in the girl's life she looks stunned, though not pissed at me like I expected, maybe even a little sympathetic.

"You blame yourself for what happened to him?" she looks back at me confused.

"I made so many bad choices that night. I ignored a call not just from a brother of this club. But from my best friend. I would have got there quicker if I hadn't come here to get help, I was too fucking cowardly," I admit for the first time ever.

"If I'd have answered that phone, if I'd done what he said instead of wasting time and coming here first. He might still be here." My foot taps the floor in frustration and my muscles tense. "And among all that, I brought Beth here, I put her in danger too when I should have left her at home." I look away, not wanting Mia to see the tears in my eyes.

"I was a kid back then. I'd just turned twenty-one, and just got the cut. I didn't know any better. I didn't trust myself to be able to take care of her or be someone this club could depend on. So I went nomad, the only person I could let down then was myself.

But all this marriage shit made me realize I love her too much to let her go."

When I look back at her, her eyes are glassy with tears and she nods back, like she's heard enough to be convinced. "I swear if she gives me another chance I won't hurt her again. You got my word," I promise.

Mia sinks back in the chair, taking in everything I've just confessed. "You ever speak to Dec about this?" she asks.

"Us guys ain't big feeling talkers," I huff a laugh. "He would never blame me even if he knew it was my fault. Look, Mia, I got to go and find Beth." I stand up and head for the door again desperate to speak to her and explain, but before I can make it Mia rushes at me and wraps her arms around my waist, squeezing me tight and shocking the hell out of me.

"Levi, what happened to Ryan wasn't your fault," she whispers. I've heard it a hundred times before but still the words carry no weight.

"I appreciate that, Mia, but…"

"It wasn't your fault, Levi. It was mine."

Slowly I turn around and the strong sassy girl I've always known suddenly looks broken.

"What you sayin'?" I look down at her confused.

"That night, Ryan was at The Casket because of me." I laugh, not because I find anything funny but because I don't know what the fuck she's trying to tell me.

"I'd been seeing someone, and I really thought he liked me."

"Seeing who?" I interrupt, hoping she ain't gonna give me the answer I'm predicting.

"His name was Vince. He was a Fallen Saints."

"Yeah Mia, I remember the guy, from when I put a fucking knife through his throat. What the fuck?"

"I thought he liked me. We snuck around and spent a lot of time together. I knew Dad and Dec wouldn't approve and I kinda liked having a secret, but as it turned out Vince wasn't who I thought he was. He wanted to share me with the others, started treating me like a trophy and I got scared. I played along and went to the bathroom, then I climbed out the window and called Ryan to come pick me up." Mia's crying now and I'm feeling far too much anger to comfort her.

"He came and he took me home. I begged him not to tell my dad or my brother and he promised, but he said they had to pay. And so he left and he went to find them. I don't know what happened after that, but I know it's all my fault. That I should have stopped him going. I shouldn't have been fucking with those guys in the first place…"

"You knew this whole time and you never said?"

"I couldn't, Dec would hate me, I love this club, Levi, all of you are like big brothers to me. I know I made mistakes and I've lived with that every fucking day since. But I never knew you blamed yourself for what happened, I can't be the reason you and Beth don't sort this out. You got to let it go, Ryan dying isn't on you, it's on me." I want to fucking yell at her to ask her how she could have been so selfish. But looking at her, I realize that nothing I say is gonna make her feel any worse than she already does.

She's carried this secret for as long as I've carried my guilt. And it don't really matter why Ryan went there that night, I still never came through for him.

"Go get your girl, Levi, be happy, don't let what happened cause any more pain." Mia smiles at me sadly.

"And what about you?" I check.

"It's time I spoke to Dec, tell him what happened. He's gonna hate me…"

"But he'll forgive you," I assure her. What she's done today is brave. I admire her for it and so I pull her under my arm and give her some comfort. "Ryan would want you to move on and be happy. That guy never held a grudge, he fucking loved everyone around him."

"Then ain't it about time you started taking your own advice?" She looks up at me, that sparkle in her eye glistening through her tears.

"That's exactly what I'm about to do," I assure her.

CHAPTER 13
BETH

I haven't even been at the coffee shop an hour and already I feel like a goldfish in a bowl. I'm trying to ignore the whispers and avoid the stares but I'm starting to think Mia was right and that this was a really bad idea.

My stomach flips when I hear the low rumble of a motorcycle and I know without looking out the window that it will be Levi.

I smile awkwardly at Renee when the door crashes open and he comes storming inside.

"You got to come with me, I don't want questions and no ain't an option," he tells me, ignoring the fact that the entire room has fallen silent.

"I think you should go with him," Renee steps slightly forward and whispers in my ear, "I got you covered."

"Fine," I slam down my tray and untie my apron. Moving towards him and wanting to swipe the satisfied grin right off his face when I do as he asks.

"You gonna at least tell me where we're going?" I ask him.

"It's a surprise," he tells me, almost being gentlemanly as he opens the door for me. I've barely taken a few steps outside before he pulls me back, causing my shoulders to slam into his solid chest.

"You ever run out on me like that again, I'll throw you over my shoulder and take you without asking," he warns.

I try not to smile as he saddles his bike and waits for me to jump on the back. And when I climb on behind him, I instantly remember how good it used to be taking a ride with him.

He pulls out onto the street and moves on, and I start to panic when I realize we're heading towards my house. I don't think I'm ready to face my dad yet, he was pissed as hell with me on the phone, and Levi being with me isn't gonna help at all.

So I'm relieved when just before we reach my street, Levi veers off and heads on to another one. The street is quiet and made up of bungalows that are all painted brightly with big front lawns. One of them stands out from the rest, it's unkept, the grass is overgrown and the whole place looks like it needs a makeover. That's the bungalow that Levi parks his bike in front of.

"Where are we?" I ask when he turns off his engine. He doesn't answer me. Just waits for me to hop off the back before he kicks down his stand and rests his bike.

"This was supposed to be ours." He stands beside me and takes my hand in his and I feel tears prick my eyes. I don't want to be reminded of what I lost. I want to figure a way to get past everything that's happened.

"I put a deposit on this place before Ryan died. We were gonna fix the place up together so I could ask you to marry me," he admits.

"That would have been perfect," I tell him, smiling fondly and wishing things could have been different.

"It still could be."

My head whips around to look at him and he's smiling.

"I've made every mortgage payment since I left town. The place is ours. I guess deep down I always knew I'd grow some balls and come back for you," he admits.

"Levi…"

"Wait, before you say anything, hear me out," he interrupts. "I left you because I was disappointed in myself, I didn't feel like I could take care of you. I let Ryan and the club down. I didn't want to risk doing the same with you. But I've learned that I can't have anyone else do the job, Beth. I need to be the one who takes care of you, who makes you happy and keeps you smiling. And I need you to trust that I can do that. To believe me when I tell you that I will never hurt you again."

"I always believed in you, Levi," I squeeze his hand tight in mine. "I feel so bad for making you stay that night. I thought you left town because you hated me."

"Hated you?" His eyes stretch open and he pulls my hand up to his chest. "You feel that?" he asks, his chest beating against my palm.

"You've owned it since you were sixteen years old and Mia brought you to the club.

I lost my way, I made mistakes, but not once have I ever not wanted to be with you. You're all I've ever wanted. You, and this…" his eyes flick toward the house, "It ain't what Laurie could offer you but it's close to your dad's place so you can still help out. So we can help out together. You ain't carrying all the weight no more," he tells me.

"You really think we can just pick up where we left off?" I ask.

"No," Levi shakes his head.

"You're gonna need to trust me again, and that's gonna be hard. But I'm gonna spend the rest of my life proving to you why you should."

"A lifetime's a long time," I warn him.

"Not if I got you." He drops to the ground pulling a ring out the pocket of his cut, and I struggle to swallow past the lump in my throat.

"I've had this ring burning a hole in my cut pocket for five years. I know I ain't good enough for you, that I've let you down, but there ain't no fucker out there who's gonna love you like this one does." He smiles up at me and I feel the warmth of his body spread a tingle all over my skin.

"Don't break my heart again, Levi Bridges," I warn him, holding out my hand so he can slide the ring on to my finger.

"So that's a yes?" he pushes the ring over my knuckle and stands up, pulling me in by the waist and smirking as his lips touch mine.

"It's a yes," I speak against his mouth, letting him lift me off the floor and spin me around.

"Then I better show you your house, Mrs. Bridges." He slides a hand under my thighs and I hold him tight around the neck as he carries me up the steps and onto the porch.

The windows are cracked, the whole building needs fixing up, but instantly the place feels like home, and I realize that nothing other than this could have ever made me happy. There was only ever one person destined for me and I don't care how long it took him to figure that out anymore, because now that we're together again, our two empty souls reunited, I know that there's nothing that will ever tear us apart.

The End

ALSO BY EMMA CREED

His Captive

US: https://amzn.to/35GxYDf
UK: https://amzn.to/3klppSc
CA: https://amzn.to/33CXPJr

DIRTY SOULS MC SERIES

Lost soul

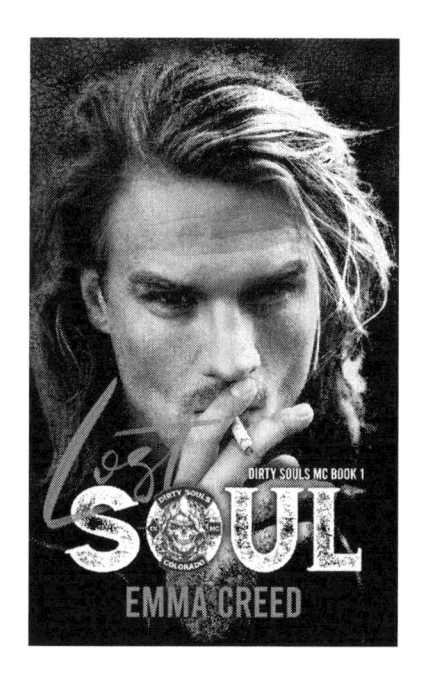

US: https://amzn.to/3rxkPF5
UK: https://amzn.to/3aOKenS
CA: https://amzn.to/2KVeoL7
AU: https://amzn.to/2JtMPbw

Reckless Soul

US: https://amzn.to/39rUnFL

UK: https://amzn.to/36mXbC0

CA: https://amzn.to/3pveo3O

AU: https://amzn.to/39xNCm1

Vengeful Soul

US: https://amzn.to/3xq7K34
UK: https://amzn.to/3sT9Epw
CA: https://amzn.to/3gzuKa4
AU: https://amzn.to/3aBs3Rs

Damaged Soul

US: https://amzn.to/3qPi2a4

UK: https://amzn.to/2UrxiOA

CA: https://amzn.to/3yupbj1

AU: https://amzn.to/3hispQF

ABOUT THE AUTHOR

Come find/stalk me on the following social media platforms.